Anne of Green Gables

By L. M. Montgomery
Adapted by Deborah Felder

Bullseye Step into Classics™

Random House 🏠 New York

Cover design by Fabia Wargin Design and Creative Media Applications, Inc.

Library of Congress Cataloging-in-Publication Data:
Felder, Deborah G.
Anne of Green Gables / by L. M. Montgomery ; adapted by Deborah Felder.
p. cm. — (Bullseye step into classics)
SUMMARY: Anne, an eleven-year-old orphan, is sent by mistake to live with a lonely,
middle-aged brother and sister on a Prince Edward Island farm and proceeds to make
an indelible impression on everyone around her.
ISBN 0-679-85467-3 (pbk.)
[1. Orphans—Fiction. 2. Friendship—Fiction. 3. Country life—Prince Edward
Island—Fiction. 4. Prince Edward Island—Fiction.] I. Montgomery, L. M. (Lucy
Maud), 1874-1942. II. Title. III. Series.
PZ7.F3356An 1994 [Fic]—dc20 93-36331

Manufactured in the United States of America 10 9 8 7 6 5 4 3 2

Contents

Chapter 1
Beginnings

It was a sunny afternoon in June. Mrs. Lynde looked out her kitchen window and saw Matthew Cuthbert drive by in a horse and buggy.

"Where is Matthew Cuthbert going?" wondered Mrs. Lynde. "And why is he wearing his best suit? He never goes visiting. He's much too quiet and shy."

Mrs. Lynde liked to know what everyone in Avonlea was doing. Matthew lived at Green Gables with his sister, Marilla. So Mrs. Lynde decided to walk over to Green Gables.

When Mrs. Lynde got to Green Gables, she found Marilla Cuthbert in the kitchen.

Marilla was a tall, thin woman with gray-streaked dark hair. It was twisted into a hard knot at the back of her head.

"Good evening, Rachel," she said. "It's a fine evening, isn't it? Won't you sit down?"

"I saw Matthew going off," Mrs. Lynde said. "I was afraid you were sick. I thought maybe he was going to get the doctor."

"Oh, no, I'm quite well. Matthew went to Bright River. We're getting a boy from the orphanage in Nova Scotia. He's coming on the train tonight."

Mrs. Lynde could not believe her ears. Marilla and Matthew adopting a boy! The world was certainly turning upside down!

"Are you serious about this, Marilla?" asked Mrs. Lynde.

"Yes, of course," Marilla said. "Matthew is getting on in years. He isn't as strong as he once was. We decided a boy could help him on the farm."

Mrs. Lynde wanted to stay until

Matthew came home with the boy. But it would be at least two hours before they arrived. She decided to go up the road and tell the surprising news to Mrs. Bell.

"I'm sorry for that poor orphan," Mrs. Lynde said when she was back out in the lane. "Matthew and Marilla don't know *anything* about raising children."

When Matthew Cuthbert arrived at the station, there was no sign of the train. The long platform was empty except for a girl sitting at the end.

The stationmaster was locking up the ticket office.

"Will the five-thirty train be along soon?" Matthew asked.

"The train's been in and gone," the stationmaster said. "But there was a passenger for you—a little girl."

"I don't understand," Matthew said. "Mrs. Spencer was supposed to send a boy, not a girl."

"Well, you'd better talk to the girl," said the stationmaster. "She's been waiting for you."

The girl watched Matthew walk toward her. She was wearing a very ugly yellowish gray dress. Beneath her faded brown sailor hat were two thick red braids. She had a small, thin, freckled face and huge gray-green eyes.

"I suppose you are Matthew Cuthbert of Green Gables?" the girl said. "I was afraid you weren't coming. I made up my mind that if you didn't come, I'd climb in that tree over there to sleep. Don't you think it would be lovely to sleep in a tree all white with moonlight?"

Matthew looked into the girl's glowing eyes. He knew he couldn't tell her there had been a mistake. He had to take her home to Green Gables.

"I'm sorry I was late," he said. "Come along. Give me your bag."

"I can carry it," the girl said. "It's got all

my worldly goods in it, but it isn't heavy."

Matthew led the way to the horse and buggy.

"It's wonderful that I'm going to live with you," the girl said. "Were you ever in an orphanage? It's worse than anything. There isn't much scope for imagination in an orphanage, believe me!"

The girl talked all the way back to Avonlea. Matthew didn't mind. He found that he liked this lively little girl.

They drove up a hill and rounded a corner. The girl pointed to one of the farms along a slope beyond the valley below. "That's Green Gables, isn't it?" she asked.

"Well, you've guessed it," Matthew said.

The girl sighed happily. "I was afraid it was only a dream. But it's real. We're nearly *home*."

Chapter 2
The Mistake

When they reached Green Gables, Marilla came forward as Matthew opened the door. When she saw the girl, she stopped in surprise.

"Matthew Cuthbert, who's *that*?" she asked. "Where's the boy?"

"There wasn't any boy," Matthew said. "There was only *her*."

He nodded at the girl.

"But we sent word to Mrs. Spencer to send a boy," Marilla said.

"Well, she sent a girl. I had to bring her home. I couldn't leave her at the station."

"You don't want me!" the girl cried out.

"I might have known it was too beautiful to last. I should have known nobody would want me!"

She sat down at the kitchen table and began to cry.

"Well, there's no need to cry about it," Marilla said.

"Yes, there *is* need!" the girl sobbed. She raised her tearstained face and looked at Marilla. "This is the most *tragical* thing that's ever happened to me!"

A smile stole across Marilla's face. "Well, don't cry any more," she said. "We're not going to send you away tonight. What's your name?"

"Would you please call me Cordelia?" the girl asked.

"Is that your name?" Marilla asked with a frown.

"No-o-o, not exactly," the girl admitted. "My real name is Anne Shirley. But I like Cordelia better. It's so much more romantic than Anne."

"Fiddlesticks!" Marilla said. "Anne is a good, sensible name."

"Well, if you call me Anne, please spell it with an *e*," Anne said. "It looks so much nicer than just plain *A-n-n*."

"All right, then, Anne spelled with an *e*, can you tell us how this mistake came to be made?" Marilla asked.

"Mrs. Spencer *distinctly* said you wanted a girl about eleven years old," Anne told her. "She kept Lily Jones for herself. Lily is five and she's very pretty. If I were pretty, would you keep me?"

"No," Marilla said. "We want a boy to help on the farm. A girl is no help."

They sat down to supper. But Anne just nibbled at her food.

"I guess she's tired," Matthew said. "Best put her to bed, Marilla."

Marilla took Anne to a bedroom in the east gable of the house. The walls of the room were bare and white. The floor was bare too, except for a round mat in the middle. There was a high bed in one corner of the room.

With a sob, Anne undressed. She put on a faded nightgown and jumped into bed. Then she pulled the covers over her head.

"Well, good night," Marilla said.

Anne's white face and big eyes appeared over the covers.

"How can you call it a *good* night?" she said. "You know it must be the very *worst* night I've ever had!"

Then she pulled the covers over her head again.

Marilla went back down to the kitchen. "The girl will have to be sent back to the orphanage," she told Matthew.

"She's a real nice little thing," Matthew said. "It's a pity to send her back. She's so set on staying."

Marilla stared at her brother. "You don't think we ought to keep her!" she said. "What help would she be?"

"We might help her," Matthew said. "And she'd be company for you."

"I don't need company," Marilla answered. "I'm not going to keep her."

"It's just as you say, of course." Matthew stood. "I'm going to bed."

Marilla put away the dishes and went to bed too. And upstairs, in the east gable, a lonely girl cried herself to sleep.

Chapter 3
Anne's History

Anne sat up in bed. She didn't know where she was. Then she remembered. This was Green Gables and they didn't want her because she wasn't a boy!

Anne jumped out of bed and knelt in front of the window to look out.

On both sides of the house were apple and cherry trees. In the garden stood lilac trees with purple flowers. Beyond the garden, a field sloped down to a brook. And past that was a hill covered with spruce and fir trees.

Anne was startled by a hand on her shoulder.

"It's time you were dressed," Marilla said.

Anne stood up. "Green Gables is so beautiful," she said. "I was imagining that I was going to stay here forever and ever."

"You'd better get dressed. Never mind your imaginings," said Marilla. "Breakfast is waiting."

Soon Anne was downstairs. Her clothes were neat. Her hair was brushed and braided. And her face was washed.

After breakfast, Anne offered to clean the dishes.

"Can you wash dishes right?" Marilla asked.

"Pretty well," Anne said. "But I'm better at looking after children. It's too bad you don't have any here for me to look after."

"I don't want any more children than I've got now," said Marilla. "*You're* problem enough. What's to be done with you, I don't know. Matthew is a silly man."

"I think he's lovely," Anne said. "I felt he was a kindred spirit as soon as I saw him."

"You're both odd, if that's what you mean," Marilla said with a sniff. "You may wash the dishes. Use plenty of hot water, and be sure to dry them well."

After Anne washed the dishes, Marilla told her she could go outside until lunch.

Anne ran to the door. But when she reached the doorway, she stopped. She turned and came back to the table.

"What's the matter now?" demanded Marilla.

"I don't dare go out," Anne said. "I won't be able to help loving all those trees and flowers and the orchard and the brook. It's so hard to keep from loving things, isn't it? I was very glad when I thought I was going to live here. I thought I'd have so many things to love. But that dream is over. So I don't think I'll go out. I'll just sit here."

Anne sat at the table until Matthew came in for lunch.

As they ate, Marilla said, "I'm going to drive to White Sands with Anne. Mrs. Spencer will probably arrange to send her back to the orphanage."

Matthew said nothing. After lunch, he hitched the horse to the buggy. Then he opened the yard gate for Marilla and Anne. Marilla looked back as the buggy bounced along. Matthew was leaning over the gate looking sadly after them.

"I've made up my mind to enjoy this drive," Anne said. "I'm not going to think about the orphanage. Are we going over the Lake of Shining Waters today?"

"We're not going over Barry's pond, if that's what you mean," Marilla said. "And if you're going to talk, you might as well tell me about yourself."

"I was eleven last March," Anne started. "I was born in Bolingbroke, Nova Scotia. My parents were Walter and

Bertha Shirley. They were teachers. They both died of a fever when I was a baby.

"No one knew what to do with me," Anne continued. "I didn't have any relatives. Finally, Mrs. Thomas said she'd take me. She was our housekeeper. I helped look after her four children—and they took a lot of looking after! When I was eight years old, Mr. Thomas died. His mother wanted Mrs. Thomas and the children, but she didn't want me."

"Then what happened?" Marilla asked.

"Then Mrs. Hammond took me because I was handy with children," Anne said. "She had eight children. *Six* of them were twins! Then Mr. Hammond died. Mrs. Hammond and her children left, so I had to go to the orphanage. It was overcrowded. But they had to take me."

"Were those women good to you?" Marilla asked.

Anne's face turned red. She looked embarrassed. "Oh, they *meant* to be," she said slowly "But they had a lot to worry about, you know. They were poor. And Mrs. Thomas' husband was drunk a lot of the time."

Marilla asked no more questions. Pity was stirring in her heart for Anne. What a terrible life she had. No wonder she longed for a real home. What if she let Anne stay at Green Gables? Matthew was set on it. And Anne seemed nice enough.

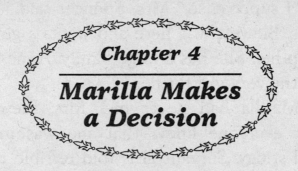

Chapter 4

Marilla Makes a Decision

Marilla and Anne finally arrived at Mrs. Spencer's house.

Mrs. Spencer came to the door with a look of surprise. "Dear, dear," she said. "You're the last folks I thought I'd see today. How are you, Anne?"

"I'm as well as can be expected, thank you," Anne said quietly.

"There's been a mistake," Marilla said. "We told Robert that we wanted a boy."

"You don't say!" said Mrs. Spencer. "Robert's daughter Nancy brought the message. She said you wanted a girl."

"Well," Marilla said, "the mistake's

been made. Won't the orphanage take Anne back?"

"I suppose so," Mrs. Spencer said. "But Mrs. Blewett was here and wants a girl to help her. She has a large family. Anne will be the very girl for her."

Marilla had never met Mrs. Blewett. But everyone knew that she was mean and stingy. Servant girls told terrible tales of her children. Marilla wasn't sure she wanted to give Anne to such a family.

"There's Mrs. Blewett now!" Mrs. Spencer cried. "How lucky. We can settle this right away."

Anne stared at Mrs. Blewett. Was she really going to be given to this unsmiling woman? Her eyes filled with tears.

"It seems there's been a mistake, Mrs. Blewett," Mrs. Spencer said. "Mr. and Miss Cuthbert wanted to adopt a boy, not a girl. Yesterday you said you needed a girl to help you. I think this one will be just right for you."

Mrs. Blewett looked at Anne from head to foot.

"If I take you," Mrs. Blewett said, "you'll have to be a good girl. Good and smart and respectful. I'll expect you to earn your keep and no mistake about that."

Mrs. Blewett turned to Marilla. "Yes, I might as well take her off your hands. If you like, I can take her right now."

Marilla looked at Anne and knew she could not give her away.

"Well, I don't know," Marilla said. "Matthew and I may want to keep Anne after all. I just came over to find out how the mistake had been made. I think I'd better take Anne home again."

Anne and Marilla climbed back into the buggy.

"Did you really say you might let me stay at Green Gables?" Anne asked. "Or did I just imagine that you did?"

"I think you'd better learn to control

that imagination of yours," Marilla said. "I haven't made a final decision yet."

"I'll do anything you want if you keep me," Anne said meekly.

When they arrived back at Green Gables, Marilla told Matthew what had happened at Mrs. Spencer's.

"I wouldn't give a dog I liked to Mrs. Blewett," Matthew said.

"I don't like her style myself," Marilla admitted. "And since you seem to want to keep Anne, I'm willing."

The next day Marilla told Anne that she could stay.

"What should I call you?" Anne asked.

"You'll just call me plain Marilla. I'm not used to being called Miss Cuthbert. It would make me nervous."

"It sounds disrespectful to just say Marilla," said Anne.

"Not if you speak respectfully," Marilla said. "Everybody in Avonlea calls me Marilla."

But Anne had another question.

"Do you think I'll have a best friend in Avonlea?" she asked. "I've dreamed of having a best friend all my life."

"Diana Barry lives nearby. She's about your age," Marilla said. "She's a very nice little girl. You'll have to behave yourself when you meet her. Mrs. Barry won't let Diana play with any girl who isn't nice and good."

Anne's face lit up. "What is Diana like?" she asked. "I hope her hair isn't red. It's bad enough to have red hair myself. I'd hate it if my best friend had red hair too."

"Diana is very pretty," Marilla said. "She has black hair and eyes and rosy cheeks. And she is good and smart. That's better than being pretty."

"I'm so glad Diana is pretty," Anne said. "Because I know I'm not pretty myself. It will be wonderful to have a beautiful best friend."

A little while later, Anne was in her room sitting on a chair by the window.

"I'm going to imagine that I'm beautiful," Anne said to herself. "I'm tall, and I'm wearing a white lace gown. There are pearls in my dark hair."

Anne ran to the mirror and looked at herself. Her freckled face and gray eyes peered back at her.

"You're not beautiful. You're only plain Anne of Green Gables," Anne said. "But it's much nicer to be Anne of Green Gables than Anne of nowhere, isn't it?"

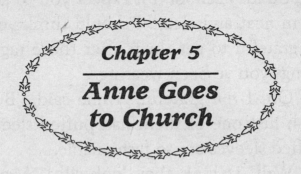

Chapter 5

Anne Goes to Church

"Well, how do you like them?" asked Marilla.

Anne looked down at the three new dresses that Marilla had made.

"I'll imagine that I like them," Anne said quietly.

"I don't want you to imagine it," Marilla said. "I can see you don't like the dresses. What's the matter with them?"

"They're—they're not *pretty*," said Anne.

"Pretty, indeed!" Marilla said with a sniff. "Those are good, sensible dresses without ruffles and frills. The brown gingham and the blue print will do for school. The black-and-white sateen is for church and Sunday school. I'll expect you to keep them neat and clean. I should think you'd be grateful to get them after those ragged things you've been wearing."

"Oh, I *am* grateful," Anne said. "But I wish just one of them had puffed sleeves. Puffed sleeves are so fashionable."

"Well, I think they look silly," Marilla said. "I like dresses to be plain and sensible. Now hang them up carefully. Then sit down and learn the Sunday-school lesson for tomorrow."

Marilla went back downstairs. Anne looked at the dresses again and sighed.

"I did hope there would be a white one with puffed sleeves," she whispered. "I'll just have to imagine that one of them has lace frills and three puffs on each sleeve."

The next morning, Marilla felt sick. So she couldn't take Anne to Sunday school.

"You'll have to go with Mrs. Lynde,"

she told Ann. "Now, behave yourself. Don't stare at people, and don't fidget. Here's a penny for the collection."

Anne started off down the lane. Along the way, she picked buttercups and wild roses. She made a big wreath of flowers and put it on her new, plain sailor hat. Anne thought the flowers made her outfit look prettier.

Mrs. Lynde wasn't home, so Anne went on to the church alone.

"Well, how did you like Sunday school?" Marilla asked when Anne came home.

Marilla did not see Anne's decorated hat. The flowers had faded, so Anne had dropped the wreath in the lane.

"I didn't like it a bit," Anne said. "It was horrid."

"Anne Shirley!" Marilla said.

"Mr. Bell's opening prayer was awfully long," Anne said. "And all the girls in my class had puffed sleeves except me."

"You shouldn't have been thinking about sleeves in Sunday school," Marilla said. "I hope you knew the lesson."

"Oh, yes," Anne said. "I answered a lot of questions. After Sunday school, Miss Rogerson showed me your pew in church. The sermon was long too. The preacher wasn't very interesting so I didn't listen much."

Deep down, Marilla agreed with Anne about Mr. Bell's prayers and the minister's sermons. She knew she ought to scold Anne for not listening in church. But somehow, she just couldn't bring herself to do it.

On Friday, Marilla went to visit Mrs. Lynde. There she heard about the flowers on Anne's hat.

"Anne," Marilla said when she came home, "Mrs. Lynde says you went to church with roses and buttercups on your hat. That was a silly thing to do."

"But lots of girls had flowers pinned on their dresses," Anne said.

"Don't answer me back, Anne," Marilla said. "Mrs. Lynde says people talked about it something dreadful. They must think I have no better sense than to let you go to church looking like that."

Anne's eyes filled with tears. "Oh, I'm so sorry. I never thought you'd mind. Lots of the girls had flowers on their hats. Maybe you'd better send me back to the orphanage. That would be terrible. But it would be better than being a trial to you."

"Nonsense," Marilla said. "I don't want to send you back to the orphanage. I just want you to behave like other little girls. Don't cry anymore. I've got some good news for you. Diana Barry came home. I'm going to borrow a pattern from her mother. If you like, you can come with me to meet Diana."

Anne stood up and clasped her hands. "Oh, Marilla, I'm scared," she whispered.

"What if Diana doesn't like me?"

"I'm sure Diana will like you," Marilla said. "It's her mother you've got to please. I hope Mrs. Barry hasn't heard about the flowers on your hat. She won't know what to think of you. You must be polite and well behaved. And don't say anything startling."

Chapter 6

A New Friend for Anne

Anne and Marilla walked over to Orchard Slope farm. Marilla knocked on the kitchen door. Mrs. Barry came to the door. She was a tall woman with black hair and black eyes.

"How do you do, Marilla," she said. "Come in. And this is the little girl you have adopted, I suppose?"

"Yes, this is Anne Shirley," said Marilla.

"Spelled with an *e*," said Anne.

Mrs. Barry shook Anne's hand. "How are you?" she asked.

"I'm well in body," Anne said. "But I'm

very rumpled in spirit, thank you, ma'am." She turned to Marilla. "That wasn't startling, was it?" she whispered.

Diana was sitting on the sofa reading a book. She dropped the book and smiled at Marilla and Anne.

"This is my little girl, Diana," said Mrs. Barry. "Diana, why don't you take Anne out to the garden? You can show her your flowers."

Anne and Diana went outside. They stood over a big clump of tiger lilies and gazed shyly at each other.

"Oh, Diana," Anne said, "do you think you can like me a little—enough to be my best friend?"

Diana laughed. "I guess so," she said. "I'm awfully glad you've come to live at Green Gables. It will be fun to have someone to play with. My sisters aren't big enough."

"Will you swear to be my best friend forever and ever?" Anne asked.

Diana looked shocked. "It's very wicked to swear," she said.

"Oh, no. Not my kind of swearing," Anne said quickly. "There are two kinds, you know."

"I've only heard of one kind of swearing," Diana said.

"My kind isn't wicked at all," Anne said. "It just means vowing and promising."

"Well, I don't mind doing that," Diana said. "How do you do it?"

Anne took hold of Diana's hands. "We join hands like this," she said. "It ought to be over running water. We'll just pretend this path is running water.

"I'll say the vow first," Anne continued. "I swear to be faithful to my best friend, Diana Barry, as long as the sun and the moon shall shine. Now you say it and put my name in."

Diana said the vow with a laugh. Then she said, "You're a funny girl, Anne. But I think I'm going to like you very much."

When Marilla and Anne started for home, Diana went with them as far as the brook. The girls promised to spend the next afternoon together.

"I'm the happiest girl on Prince Edward Island," Anne told Marilla. "Diana and I are going to build a playhouse tomorrow. She's going to lend me a book to read and teach me a new song. I wish I had something to give Diana. Did you know that I'm an inch taller than she is? But she's ever so much fatter. She said she'd like to be thin. But I think she just said that to make me feel better."

"Well, I hope you won't talk Diana to death," said Marilla. "And remember this, Anne. You're not going to play all the time. You'll have your chores to do, too. And chores come first."

Back at Green Gables Matthew had a surprise for Anne. He pulled a small bag from his pocket and handed it to her.

"I heard you say you like chocolate candies," he said. "So I got you some."

"Humph," Marilla said with a sniff. "It'll ruin her teeth and stomach. There, there, child, don't look so miserable. You can eat those, since Matthew has gone and got them. Don't get sick eating them all at once."

"I won't," said Anne. "I'll just eat one tonight. And I can give half of them to Diana, can't I? They'll taste much sweeter if I give her half. I'm so glad I have something to give her."

"I will say this for the child," Marilla said when Anne had gone up to bed. "She isn't stingy. Dear me, it's only three weeks since she came. I can't imagine the place without her. Don't be looking I-told-you-so, Matthew. I'll admit that I'm getting fond of her. But don't rub it in, Matthew Cuthbert!"

Chapter 7

Anne Goes to School

Anne started school in September. The Avonlea school was a white building with one big room. Inside were desks that opened and shut at the top.

"Marilla, I think I'm going to like school," Anne said when she came home. "I met Ruby Gillis and Tillie Boulter. But Diana is still my best friend. And Prissy Andrews told Sara Gillis that I had a very pretty nose. That's the first nice thing anyone's ever said about my looks. Is it true, Marilla? Do I have a pretty nose?"

"Your nose is nice enough," Marilla said. Secretly she thought that Anne's nose was very pretty.

Three weeks later, Anne and Diana were walking to school together as usual.

"Gilbert Blythe will be in school today," Diana said. "He's been visiting his cousins all summer. He'll be in your class. He missed a lot of school when he went out west with his father. He's in the fourth class even though he's almost fourteen."

The girls entered the schoolhouse and sat at the desk they shared.

"That's Gilbert Blythe sitting across from you, Anne," whispered Diana. "Don't you think he's *very* handsome?"

Anne looked across the aisle. Gilbert Blythe was a tall boy with curly brown hair and a teasing smile. Gilbert looked at Anne and winked.

"He *is* handsome," Anne whispered to Diana. "I think he's very bold, though. It isn't good manners to wink at a stranger."

But it wasn't until the afternoon that things really began to happen.

Mr. Phillips was in the back of the

room helping Prissy with a math problem. No one else was studying. They were eating apples, whispering to each other, or drawing pictures on their slates.

Gilbert was trying to make Anne look at him. But Anne was gazing out the window and daydreaming.

Gilbert wasn't used to being ignored by a girl. So he picked up the end of Anne's long red braid. Then he said in a loud whisper, "Carrots! Carrots!"

Anne turned and glared at him. She jumped to her feet.

"How dare you!" she shouted.

And then—*thwack!* Anne hit Gilbert over the head with her slate.

Mr. Phillips marched down the aisle. "Anne Shirley, what does this mean?" he asked.

Anne didn't answer. She wouldn't tell everyone she had been called "carrots."

"It was my fault," Gilbert said. "I teased her."

Mr. Phillips paid no attention to

Gilbert. "I am sorry to see a student of mine display such a temper," he said. "Anne, go stand at the blackboard."

Anne did not cry or hang her head. She was still too angry.

After school Anne marched out with her head held high. Gilbert hurried up to her.

"I'm sorry I made fun of your hair, Anne," he said. "Honest. Don't be mad."

But Anne just swept right past him.

"Oh, how could you, Anne?" Diana asked as they walked down the road together.

"I will never forgive Gilbert Blythe," Anne said.

"But Gilbert makes fun of all the girls," Diana said. "He laughs at my hair because it's so black. He calls me a crow."

"Being called carrots is worse," said Anne. "Gilbert Blythe has hurt my feelings *terribly*, Diana."

But that was just the beginning.

Chapter 8
Gilbert Blythe

"Everyone has been coming back from lunch too late," Mr. Phillips said the next day. "From now on, you must be in your seats when I return."

At lunchtime, everyone went to Mr. Bell's spruce grove. Anne was at the far end of the grove. She was wandering around singing softly to herself.

Suddenly Jimmy Glover shouted, "Master's coming!"

The girls got to the schoolhouse just in time. But the boys had to climb down from the trees. Anne ran as fast as she could. She caught up with the boys at the door. Anne and the boys entered the room as Mr. Phillips hung up his hat.

Anne dropped into her seat, gasping for breath.

Mr. Phillips didn't want to bother punishing twelve students for being late. But he had to punish someone.

"Anne Shirley," he said, "since you seem to like the boys' company so much, we shall let you have more of it. Go sit with Gilbert Blythe."

The other boys snickered. Diana turned pale. Anne just stared.

"Did you hear what I said, Anne?" Mr. Phillips asked.

"Yes, sir," Anne said slowly. "But I didn't think you really meant it."

"I did mean it," said Mr. Phillips.

For a moment Anne looked as if she were going to disobey him. Then she stood up and stepped across the aisle. She sat down beside Gilbert Blythe and buried her face in her arms on the desk.

The children whispered and giggled and nudged each other. But they soon went back to work.

When nobody was looking, Gilbert took a little pink candy heart from his desk. The heart had *You Are Sweet* written on it. Gilbert slipped the heart under the curve of Anne's arm.

Anne lifted her head. She took the pink heart between her fingertips and dropped it on the floor. She crushed the heart with the heel of her shoe. Then she buried her face in her arms again.

After school had ended, Anne went over to her desk. She took out her books, writing tablet, pen and ink, and arithmetic. Then she piled them neatly on her cracked slate.

"Why are you taking all those things home, Anne?" Diana wanted to know when they were out on the road.

"I'm not going back," said Anne.

Diana stared at her. "Will Marilla let

you stay home?" she asked.

"She'll have to," said Anne. "I'll *never* go to school again."

"Oh, Anne!" Diana said. "What will I do? Mr. Phillips will make me sit with that awful Gertie Pye. I know he will because she's sitting alone. Please come back to school, Anne."

"I'd do almost anything in the world for you, Diana," Anne said sadly. "But I can't do this, so please don't ask me."

"But think of all the fun you'll miss," Diana said. "We're playing ball next week. And you've never played ball before, Anne. It's very exciting. We're going to learn a new song, too. And we're going to read a new book out loud by the brook. You love to read out loud, Anne."

But Anne's mind was made up. She would not go to school again. When she got home, she told Marilla.

"Nonsense," said Marilla.

"It isn't nonsense at all," Anne said.

"Don't you understand? I've been insulted."

"Insulted, fiddlesticks! You'll go to school tomorrow as usual."

"Oh, no." Anne shook her head. "I'm not going back, Marilla. I'll learn my lessons at home. I'll be as good as I can be. But I will not go back to school!"

Marilla decided not to say anything more about school just then. Instead, she went to ask Mrs. Lynde what to do.

"Well," Mrs. Lynde said, "I'd let her stay home for a little while, that's what. She'll cool off and decide to go back on her own. The less fuss made the better, in my opinion."

Marilla took Mrs. Lynde's advice. Not another word was said to Anne about going back to school. She learned her lessons at home, did her chores, and played with Diana.

But Anne had made up her mind to hate Gilbert Blythe for the rest of her life.

Chapter 9
The Tea Party

"I'm going to a meeting." Marilla said to Anne one Saturday morning in October. "If you like, you can ask Diana to come over. She can spend the afternoon and have tea."

"Oh, thank you," Anne said happily. "I've longed to have Diana come to tea."

"You can open the little jar of cherry preserves and have it with your cake and cookies," Marilla said. "And there's half a bottle of raspberry cordial left over from the church social. It's on the second shelf of the sitting-room closet. You and Diana can have it if you like."

After Marilla had driven off, Diana

came over. She was wearing her second-best dress. She knocked primly on the front door.

Anne, wearing *her* second-best dress, opened the door. The two girls shook hands as if they were meeting each other for the first time. Diana put her hat in Anne's room. Then the girls sat in the sitting room.

"How is your mother?" Anne asked, trying to sound grown-up.

"She is very well, thank you," Diana said. "Is Mr. Cuthbert hauling potatoes down to the ship this afternoon?"

"Yes," Anne said. "Our potato crop is very good this year. I hope your father's crop is too."

"It is fairly good, thank you," Diana said. "Have you picked many apples yet?"

"Oh, ever so many," Anne said. Then she forgot to act grown-up and jumped to her feet. "Let's go out to the orchard and pick the rest of the apples."

They picked and ate apples until Diana

started to talk about Gilbert Blythe. Anne didn't want to hear about him, so she said it was time to go back and have some raspberry cordial.

Anne finally found a bottle marked *Raspberry Cordial* at the back of the top shelf. She put the bottle on a tray with a glass.

"Help yourself, Diana," Anne said. "I don't want any after all those apples."

Diana poured herself a big glass of cordial and sipped it.

"It's awfully good, Anne," she said. "I didn't know raspberry cordial was so good."

"I'm glad you like it," Anne said. "Drink as much as you want."

Diana drank a second big glass of cordial. Then she drank a third.

"This cordial is much better than Mrs. Lynde's," Diana said. "It doesn't taste a bit like hers."

"Of course Marilla's is better," Anne said. "Marilla is a famous cook. She's trying to teach me. But I'm a great trial to her. One time I found a drowned mouse in the plum-pudding sauce! I took the mouse out. But I forgot to ask Marilla what to do with the sauce until she brought it to the table. Then I remembered the mouse, so I shrieked, 'Don't use the sauce, Marilla! A mouse drowned in it!' And we had company, too! What's the matter, Diana?"

Diana stood up unsteadily. Then she sat down and put her hands to her head.

"I'm—I'm awful sick," she said. "I—I want to go home."

"But you can't go home without having tea!" cried Anne. "I'll get it ready right now."

"I'm dizzy," Diana said. "I want to go home."

Anne got Diana's hat and walked with her as far as the Barry yard fence. Then Anne cried all the way back to Green Gables. Her tea party had been a disaster.

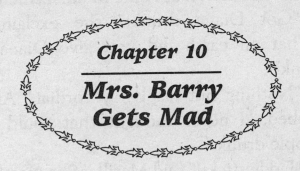

Chapter 10

Mrs. Barry Gets Mad

It rained all day Sunday, so Anne couldn't go out to play with Diana. On Monday afternoon, Marilla sent her to Mrs. Lynde's on an errand.

Soon Anne came running back up the lane, crying. She dashed into the kitchen and flung herself on the sofa.

"Whatever is wrong now, Anne?" asked Marilla.

Anne sat up. "Mrs. Lynde went to visit Mrs. Barry today," she wailed. "And Mrs. Barry said I got Diana *drunk* on Saturday. She said I'm a bad little girl. She's not going to let Diana play with me ever again."

Marilla stared at Anne in amazement.

"Got Diana drunk!" she exclaimed. "What on earth did you give Diana to drink?"

"Nothing but raspberry cordial," Anne sobbed. "I never thought that could get people drunk."

"Fiddlesticks!" said Marilla. She marched to the sitting-room pantry. There on the shelf was the bottle marked *Raspberry Cordial.*

It was the bottle Marilla had used for some of her famous homemade currant wine. Marilla remembered that she had put the bottle of raspberry cordial in the cellar instead of in the pantry, as she had told Anne.

She went back to the kitchen, chuckling a little in spite of herself.

"Anne, you certainly know how to get yourself in trouble. You gave Diana currant wine instead of cordial. Couldn't you tell it wasn't cordial?"

"I didn't taste it," said Anne. "Oh, Marilla, Mrs. Barry thinks I did it on purpose!"

"There, there, child, don't cry," Marilla said. "You weren't to blame. Just go to Mrs. Barry and tell her it was an accident."

"I don't think I could face Diana's mother," Anne said with a sigh. "I wish you'd go, Marilla. She might listen to you."

"Well, I will," Marilla said. "Don't cry any more, Anne. It will be all right."

But it wasn't all right. Anne could tell that from Marilla's face when she came home.

"Mrs. Barry won't forgive me, will she?" Anne asked sadly.

"Mrs. Barry indeed!" snapped Marilla. "Of all the unreasonable women I ever saw, she's the worst. I told her it was a mistake and you weren't to blame. But she simply didn't believe me." With that, she marched off into the kitchen.

Marilla slipped into Anne's room later that night. She saw that Anne had cried herself to sleep.

"Poor little girl," Marilla murmured. She lifted a loose curl of hair from Anne's face. Then she bent down and gently kissed Anne's flushed cheek.

The next morning, Anne came downstairs carrying her schoolbooks and slate.

"I'm going back to school," she announced. "That's all there is left for me now that my best friend is gone forever."

Marilla was surprised but glad that Anne had finally decided to go to school again.

The girls welcomed Anne with open arms. They had missed her. Ruby Gillis passed three plums over to her. Ella May MacPherson gave her a huge paper pansy. Katie Boulter gave her an empty bottle to keep scented water in.

The girls weren't the only ones who

were glad to see Anne. After lunch, Anne found a big apple on her desk. She was about to take a bite when she remembered that kind of apple only grew in the Blythe orchard. Gilbert Blythe had left the apple on her desk.

Anne dropped the apple as if it were a red-hot piece of coal. Then she wiped her hands on her handkerchief.

Still, Anne was happy to be back at school with her friends. But she had to sit with Minnie Andrews. She missed Diana very much.

"Diana might have smiled at me once, I think," Anne said to Marilla that night.

But the next morning, a note and a small package were passed to Anne. The note read:

Dear Anne,
Mother says I'm not to play with you or talk to you even in school. It isn't my fault and don't be mad at me. I miss you and I don't

like Gertie Pye one bit. I made you a book-mark out of red tissue paper. They're very fashionable right now. Only three girls in school know how to make them. When you look at it, remember your true friend,

Diana Barry

Anne wrote back:

My own darling Diana,
Of course I'm not mad at you because you have to obey your mother. I will keep your present forever. Minnie Andrews is nice, even though she has no imagination. But after having been your best friend, I cannot be Minnie's.

Yours forever,
Anne or Cordelia Shirley
P.S. I'll sleep with your letter under my pillow tonight.

Chapter 11

Anne to the Rescue

Anne made up her mind to work hard in school. She wanted to be the best student in her class. But so did Gilbert Blythe.

A rivalry sprang up between them. They tried to beat each other in every subject. One day, Anne would be the best student. The next day, it would be Gilbert.

At the end of the term, Anne and Gilbert were promoted to the fifth class. They began to study new subjects. The hardest math subject for Anne to learn was geometry.

"It's awful stuff, Marilla," Anne said with a groan. "Mr. Phillips says I'm terrible at it. And Gil—I mean, some of the others are so smart at it. Even Diana. Oh, Marilla, I miss Diana so much."

One snowy January evening, Anne was studying at the kitchen table. Matthew was dozing on the sofa. Marilla had gone to Charlottetown to see the premier of Canada.

Anne really wanted to read a book. But if she stopped studying, Gilbert would beat her in geometry tomorrow.

Suddenly she heard the sound of running footsteps on the icy walk outside. The door was flung open and in rushed Diana Barry.

"What's happened, Diana?" Anne cried. "Has your mother forgiven me?"

"Oh, Anne, come quick," Diana pleaded. "My little sister is awfully sick. She's got croup. And Mother and Father are in Charlottetown. Mother hired Mary

Joe to look after us while she's gone But Mary Joe doesn't know anything about croup. Oh, Anne, I'm so scared!"

Without a word, Matthew got up and reached for his cap and coat. He slipped past Diana and into the yard.

"He's gone to get the doctor," Anne said as she put on her jacket.

"But all the doctors are probably in Charlottetown," sobbed Diana.

"Don't cry, Diana," Anne said. "I know exactly what to do. Don't forget—I took care of three pairs of Hammond twins. They had croup all the time. I'll just get some medicine. You might not have any at your house."

The girls went out into the frosty night and hurried over to Diana's house.

Three-year-old Minnie May was feverish. Her hoarse breathing could be heard all over the house.

"First, we need lots of hot water," Anne said. "There, I've filled up the kettle. Mary

Joe, put some wood in the stove. It seems to me you might have thought of that before if you had any imagination. Diana, you try to find some soft cloths."

Anne gave Minnie May a dose of medicine. Then she undressed the little girl and put her to bed.

Anne and Diana sat with Minnie May all through the night. Anne gave her every drop of medicine in the bottle.

It was three in the morning before Matthew arrived with the doctor. He had gone all the way to Spencervale to find one. But by now, Minnie May was much better and fast asleep. A very tired Anne went home with Matthew.

It was the middle of the afternoon before Anne woke up. She dressed and went downstairs. Marilla had come home and was sitting in the kitchen knitting.

"Your lunch is in the oven," she said. "And there's plum preserve in the pantry. You must be hungry. Matthew told me about last night. Never mind talking until you've eaten."

After Anne had finished her plums, Marilla said, "Mrs. Barry was here this afternoon, Anne. She wanted to see you, but I wouldn't wake you up. She says you saved Minnie May's life. The doctor said so too. Mrs. Barry is sorry for the way she acted about the currant wine. She knows now you didn't mean to get Diana drunk. She hopes you'll forgive her and be friends with Diana again. You're to go over there this evening."

Anne's face shone with happiness.

"Marilla, can I go right now?" she asked. "I'll wash the dishes when I get back."

"Yes, yes, run along," Marilla said, shaking her head.

Anne ran out into the cold without even putting on her jacket.

Chapter 12

The Sleepover

"Oh, Marilla," Anne said one February evening. "Tomorrow is Diana's birthday. Her mother said I can spend the night. In the spare room! Before that, we're going to the school concert. Oh, please say you'll let me go, Marilla!"

Marilla finally agreed.

The next night Anne and Diana drove to the concert in a sleigh with Diana's cousins.

Anne loved every performance except one. When Gilbert Blythe began his poem, Anne read a book until he had finished.

The girls got back to Diana's house

late. Everybody seemed to be asleep. The girls tiptoed into the long parlor next to the spare room.

"Let's change in here," said Diana. "It's nice and warm."

They put on their nightgowns. Then Anne said, "Let's race and see who gets to bed first."

The girls ran through the parlor and through the spare-room door. They jumped on the bed at the same time.

Something moved under the covers. There was a gasp and a cry. A voice said: "Merciful goodness!"

Anne and Diana raced back out of the room and up the stairs.

"Who—or what—was that?" whispered Anne.

"It was Aunt Josephine," Diana said, laughing. "She's father's aunt from Charlottetown. She's seventy and very prim and proper. Well, we'll have to sleep with Minnie May—and she kicks!"

Miss Josephine Barry did not come to

breakfast the next morning. After breakfast, Anne hurried home. In the afternoon, she went to Mrs. Lynde's on an errand.

"So you and Diana scared poor old Miss Barry half to death last night," Mrs. Lynde said. "Diana's mother told me that old Miss Barry has a terrible temper. She wouldn't speak to Diana at all."

"It wasn't Diana's fault," Anne said. "It was mine. I suggested racing to see who would get into bed first."

"I knew it had to be your idea," said Mrs. Lynde. "Well, it's made a lot of trouble. Miss Barry was going to stay a month. But now she's leaving tomorrow. She had promised to pay for Diana's music lessons, but she's changed her mind. The Barrys are very upset. Miss Barry is rich, and they want to stay on her good side."

Anne ran over to Diana's house. Diana met her at the kitchen door.

"I heard that Miss Barry is very angry and won't stay," Anne said. "Why didn't you tell her it was my fault?"

"I could never do that," Diana said. "I'm not a tattletale. Anyhow, I was just as much to blame as you."

"Well, I'm going to tell Miss Barry myself," Anne said. She walked up to the sitting-room door and knocked.

"Come in," a voice said sharply.

Anne entered the room. Miss Josephine Barry was sitting by the fire knitting. She glared at Anne through her gold-rimmed glasses.

"Who are you?" Miss Barry demanded.

"I'm Anne of Green Gables," said Anne. "And I've come to confess."

"Confess what?" Miss Barry snapped.

"That it was all my fault about jumping into bed on you," Anne said. "It was my idea to jump into bed. So you mustn't blame Diana."

"Oh, I mustn't, eh?" said Miss Barry. "Well, Diana did her share of the jumping."

"It was only in fun," Anne said. "I think

you ought to forgive us. Anyway, please forgive Diana and let her have her music lessons. If you have to be mad at someone, be mad at me."

Miss Barry stopped glaring. "How would you like it if you were woken up out of a sound sleep by two girls jumping on you?" she asked.

"It must have been terrible," said Anne. "But imagine how we felt, Miss Barry. We didn't know anybody was in that bed. You scared us, too. And we couldn't sleep in the spare room after being promised. You're probably used to sleeping in spare rooms. But what if you were a little orphan girl who was going to sleep in a spare room for the first time?"

Miss Barry began to laugh. "I'm afraid my imagination is a little rusty," she said. "It's been so long since I used it. Now sit down and tell me about yourself."

"I'm sorry I can't," Anne said. "I have to go home. But before I go, I wish you would forgive Diana. And I wish you would stay."

Miss Barry smiled. "Maybe I will, if you'll come over and talk to me."

That evening, Miss Barry told Diana's parents that she had unpacked her bag.

"I've made up my mind to stay," she said. "I want to get to know that Anne girl better. She makes me laugh."

Miss Barry stayed even longer than a month. And when she finally left, she said, "Remember, Anne girl, when you come to town, you're to visit me. You can sleep in my very best spare-room bed."

Chapter 13

Anne Takes a Dare

That August, Diana had a party for the girls in her class. They decided to play a new game called "daring."

Josie Pye went first.

"Jane Andrews," she said, "I dare you to hop once around the garden on one leg without stopping."

Jane lost the dare. She could only hop to the second corner of the garden.

Then Anne dared Josie Pye to walk along the top of the board fence. Josie did it very quickly and easily.

"I don't think it's so great to walk a

little board fence," Anne said. "I knew a girl who could walk the top of a roof."

"I don't believe it," snapped Josie. "I don't believe anybody could walk on the top of a roof. *You* couldn't, anyhow."

"I bet I could!" Anne cried.

"Then I dare you to climb up there and walk on the top of the Barrys' kitchen roof!" Josie said.

Anne turned pale. But she walked to the ladder leaning against the kitchen roof.

The girls followed Anne. They couldn't believe she was really going to do it.

"You'll fall off and be killed," Diana said.

"I have to do it," Anne said. "My honor is at stake. If I am killed, Diana, you may have my pearl bead ring."

No one moved as Anne climbed the ladder. She balanced on the top of the roof and began to walk. She took five or six steps.

Then it happened.

Anne began to sway. She lost her balance and fell. Then she slid down the roof and hit the ground.

Diana and the other girls rushed to the other side of the house where Anne had fallen.

Diana knelt down. "Anne, are you killed?" she shrieked. "Anne, speak to me!"

Anne sat up dizzily. "No, Diana, I am not killed," she said shakily. "But I think I am unconscious."

"Where?" sobbed Carrie Sloane. "Oh, where, Anne?"

Before Anne could answer, Mrs. Barry arrived on the scene. Anne tried to get to her feet. But she sank back with a cry.

"What's the matter? Where have you hurt yourself?" asked Mrs. Barry.

"My ankle," Anne gasped. "Oh, I can't walk home. I don't think I could hop there on one foot!"

Marilla was out in the orchard when

she saw Mr. Barry coming up the slope toward her, carrying Anne.

At that moment Marilla knew how much she loved Anne. She knew that Anne was dearer to her than anything on earth.

She hurried down the slope.

"Mr. Barry, what has happened to her?" she gasped.

Anne lifted her head and said, "Don't be scared, Marilla. I was walking the top of the Barrys' roof and fell off. I think I sprained my ankle. But let's look on the bright side. I might have broken my neck."

Marilla led the way to the kitchen. "Bring her in here, Mr. Barry, and lay her on the sofa. Mercy me! The child's fainted!"

Matthew came in from the harvest field and went to get the doctor. The doctor said that Anne had broken her ankle.

Later, Marilla went up to Anne's room with a tray of food. Anne was lying in bed, her ankle in a cast.

"Don't you feel sorry for me, Marilla?" Anne asked in a small voice.

"It was your own fault," Marilla said. She pulled down the blind and lit the lamp.

"But what would *you* have done if someone dared you to walk the top of a roof?" asked Anne.

"I would have stayed on the ground and let them dare away," said Marilla. "Such nonsense!"

Anne sighed. "I'm not as strong willed as you are," she said. "I had to take Josie Pye's dare. If I didn't, she would never have let me forget it. Anyway, please don't be mad at me. I won't be able to walk for six or seven weeks. And Gil—I mean, everybody will get ahead of me in class. I feel very sorry for myself. But I'll try to be brave if you won't be mad at me, Marilla."

"There, there, I'm not mad," Marilla

said. "Go ahead and eat your supper."

Anne had many visitors over the next seven weeks. Her friends brought her flowers and books. They told her all the news at school.

"Everybody has been so nice to me, Marilla," Anne said. "Even Josie Pye came over. I think she was sorry she dared me to walk the roof. And Diana told me all about our new teacher. Her name is Miss Muriel Stacy. She has blond hair and blue eyes. And the puffs on her sleeves are the biggest in Avonlea. She has everyone recite poems or plays on Friday afternoons. And she takes everyone outside to study plants and birds. I can't wait to go back to school. I just know I'm going to like her."

Marilla smiled and shook her head. "Well, there's one thing I know for sure," she said. "Your fall off the Barry roof hasn't injured your tongue at all!"

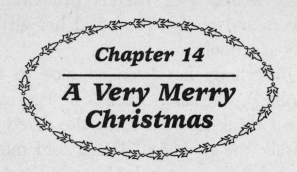

Chapter 14
A Very Merry Christmas

Anne went back to school in October. A month later, the Avonlea students began to plan a Christmas concert. It was Miss Stacy's idea. Anne was very excited about the concert. Marilla thought it was all nonsense.

"I don't approve of these concerts," she grumbled. "They fill children's heads with foolishness. You should be busy learning your lessons."

"But it's for a good cause," Anne said. "We want to raise money for a school-house flag."

"Fiddlesticks!" said Marilla. "All you

want is to have a good time."

"Well, it *is* fun planning a concert," Anne said. "Diana is singing a song. I'm going to be in two little plays. And I'm reciting two poems. Oh, Marilla, I know you're not as excited about the concert as I am. But don't you hope I'll make you proud of me?"

"All I hope is that you behave yourself," said Marilla. "I'll be very glad when all this fuss is over and you settle down again."

Anne sighed. Then she went out to the backyard, where Matthew was chopping wood.

Anne talked to him about the concert.

"Well, I reckon it's going to be a pretty good concert. And I expect you'll do your part just fine," he said, smiling.

Anne smiled back at him. She was glad she had come out to talk to Matthew. He always made her feel better.

One cold, gray December evening,

Matthew came into the kitchen. He sat down in the woodbox corner to take off his boots.

Anne and her friends were practicing for the concert, laughing and talking.

For the first time, Matthew noticed that Anne was not dressed like the other girls. They were all wearing pretty, brightly colored dresses. He wondered why Marilla made Anne wear such plain, dark dresses.

"I'm going to give Anne a nice new dress for Christmas," Matthew thought.

He decided to ask Mrs. Lynde to help him.

"Pick out a dress for you to give Anne?" said Mrs. Lynde. "I'll be happy to. I think a nice rich brown would just suit Anne. I'll sew it up, too, if you like."

"Well, I'm much obliged," said Matthew. "And—and—I think they make the sleeves different now. If it wouldn't be too much trouble, I'd like them made the new way."

"You mean puffs? Of course. Don't worry about a thing," said Mrs. Lynde. "I know just what to do. I'll make the dress in the very latest style."

On Christmas morning, Anne came running downstairs.

"Merry Christmas, Marilla! Merry Christmas, Matthew!" Anne shouted.

Matthew unfolded the dress from its paper wrappings.

"Why—why—Matthew, is that for me?" Anne asked.

She took the pretty brown dress and held it up. Her eyes were shining. The dress was soft and silky. It had a lace ruffle on the collar. And it had puffed sleeves.

"That's a Christmas present for you," Matthew said. "Why, Anne, you're crying. Don't you like it?"

Anne laid the dress over a chair. She smiled at Matthew. "*Like* it? Oh, Matthew, I love it! Thank you. It's perfect. Look at those sleeves!"

"Well, well, let's have breakfast," said Marilla. "I didn't think you needed a new dress. But Matthew got it for you, so take good care of it. Mrs. Lynde left you a hair ribbon to match."

After breakfast, Anne met Diana at the bridge in the hollow.

"I've got something for you from Aunt Josephine," said Diana.

She handed Anne a box.

Anne opened the box. Inside was a card and a pair of little leather slippers. They had beaded toes, satin bows, and shiny buckles.

"Oh, Diana," said Anne. "This is the best Christmas I've ever had!"

The Christmas concert was held that night. After it was over, Anne and Diana walked home together under the starry sky.

"Everybody just loved your recitations," said Diana. "And when you ran off the stage, one of the roses fell out of your hair. I saw Gilbert Blythe pick it up and put it in his pocket. That's so romantic. Aren't you pleased?"

"No," Anne said. "I don't care what that person does. And I never will."

Chapter 15

No More Red Hair

One April evening when Marilla got home Anne wasn't in the kitchen.

Marilla went to Anne's room to get a candle. Anne was lying facedown on the bed.

"Goodness!" Marilla exclaimed "Have you been asleep?"

"No," Anne said into the pillows.

"Are you sick?" Marilla asked.

"No. Please go away and don't look at me," Anne said.

"Whatever is the matter with you?" Marilla asked. "What have you done? Get up this minute and tell me."

Anne sat up. "Look at my hair, Marilla," she whispered.

Marilla lifted her candle and looked. Then she gasped in surprise.

"Anne Shirley, what have you done to your hair? It's *green!*"

"Yes, it's green," Anne moaned. "I thought nothing could be worse than red hair. But now I know it's ten times worse to have green hair."

"But how did it get to be green?" asked Marilla.

"I dyed it."

"Dyed it! Dyed your hair! Anne Shirley, that was a terrible thing to do!"

"I know," Anne admitted. "But I thought my hair would look beautiful. I bought the dye from a peddler. He said it would turn my hair raven black."

"Well, come down to the kitchen and we'll wash your hair," said Marilla. "Maybe we can wash out the dye."

But the dye didn't come out. Anne would not leave the house. She washed her hair every day for a week. But it was still green.

"It's no use," Marilla said. "I'll have to cut your hair. You can't stay home from school any longer."

Marilla cut Anne's hair very short. Nobody made fun of Anne's short hair at school. Nobody except Josie Pye.

"Josie said I look like a scarecrow," Anne told Marilla. "I wanted to say something mean back to her. But I didn't. I forgave her instead. Am I talking too much, Marilla? Does it hurt your head?"

"My head feels better now," said Marilla. "I don't mind your talk. I'm used to it."

Which was Marilla's way of saying that she liked to hear it.

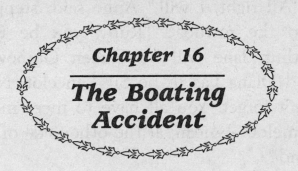

Chapter 16

The Boating Accident

One summer day Anne, Diana, Ruby, and Jane were standing by the Lake of Shining Waters. They were going to act out a story about King Arthur and his knights.

The girls were deciding who should play Elaine. Elaine was the beautiful maiden who died for the love of the handsome knight Sir Lancelot.

It was Anne's idea to act out the story. She thought it would be very romantic.

"Now, after Elaine dies," Anne said, "she floats to Camelot in a barge. Your father's rowboat can be the barge, Diana."

"You have to be Elaine, Anne," said

Diana. "I'm too scared to float down the pond in a boat."

"All right, I will," Anne said, stepping into the rowboat. "Ruby, you be King Arthur. Jane will be Queen Guinevere. And Diana has to be Sir Lancelot. Now, don't forget. You all have to meet me at Camelot—I mean, at the other side of the pond."

Anne lay down on the bottom of the boat and closed her eyes. She folded her hands across her chest.

"Now push the boat into the pond," Jane told the other girls.

The girls pushed. The boat floated out into the current.

Anne drifted down the pond. She pretended that she was Elaine, the maiden who had loved Sir Lancelot.

Suddenly Anne felt water underneath her. She opened her eyes and sat up. She looked down and saw a big crack in the bottom of the boat. Water was pouring through the crack. The boat was sinking!

The boat floated toward the log bridge and bumped into one of the pilings made out of old tree trunks. Anne quickly climbed up on one of the tree trunks and grabbed onto a little branch above it.

The boat drifted under the bridge and sank.

Diana, Ruby, and Jane saw the boat sink and thought that Anne had sunk with it. They stared at the pond in horror. Then they started running through the woods, screaming at the top of their lungs. They never stopped to look toward the bridge.

Anne heard their screams and saw them running across the main road.

"Oh, please bring help soon," she whispered. She wasn't sure how much longer she could hold on to the little branch.

Each minute seemed like an hour.

"Oh, why doesn't somebody come?" Anne thought.

Just when she thought she couldn't hang on another minute, someone came rowing toward her. It was Gilbert Blythe.

He rowed up and held out his hand. Anne didn't want to take his hand. But she had to. She clung to his hand and scrambled into the boat.

"What happened, Anne?" asked Gilbert.

"We were playing Elaine," Anne said without looking at him. "And I had to drift down to Camelot in the barge—I mean, the rowboat. The boat began to leak and I climbed up here. Would you be kind enough to row me to the landing?"

When they reached the landing, Anne stepped out of the boat onto the shore.

"Thank you very much," she said stiffly. She turned away.

Gilbert jumped out of the boat and took her arm.

"Look, Anne," he said. "Can't we be friends? I'm awfully sorry I made fun of your hair that time. Besides, it happened so long ago I think your hair is very pretty now."

He looked down at her, and Anne's heart skipped a beat.

But then she remembered how much he had hurt her feelings when he called her "carrots." And because of him, she had been disgraced in front of the whole school. She would never forgive him!

"No," she said coldly. "I'll never be friends with you, Gilbert Blythe!"

"All right!" Gilbert jumped back into his boat. "I'll never ask you to be friends again, Anne Shirley!"

He rowed away. Anne held her head high. But she knew she had been wrong not to forgive Gilbert this time.

Halfway up the path, Anne met Diana and Jane. "Anne!" Diana gasped. "We thought you had drowned. How did you escape?"

"I climbed up on one of the pilings,"

Anne said wearily. "And Gilbert Blythe came along and rowed me to shore."

"Oh, that's so romantic," Jane said. "Of course you'll speak to him after this."

"Of course I won't," Anne said.

Later Anne told Marilla, "I'm going to give up being romantic. I thought it would be romantic to dye my hair black and to pretend I was Elaine. But my hair turned green and I almost drowned. So I'd rather be sensible and stay out of trouble. I think you're going to see a more sensible Anne from now on, Marilla."

"I certainly hope so," said Marilla.

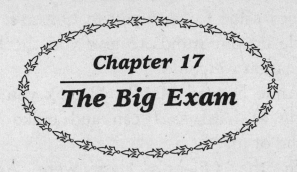

Chapter 17
The Big Exam

"Anne," Marilla said one night in November, "Miss Stacy was here today."

Anne was lying on the hearth rug gazing into the fire. She looked up at Marilla.

"Oh, I'm sorry I was out," Anne said. "Why was Miss Stacy here?"

"She came to ask me if Matthew and I wanted you to join the class that is going to be studying for the entrance exam into Queen's Academy. What do you think? Would you like to go to Queen's and study to be a teacher?"

"Oh, yes," Anne said. "I'd love to be a teacher. But won't it be too expensive to send me to Queen's?"

"Don't worry about that," said Marilla "Matthew and I decided to put some money aside to send you to Queen's. We made up our minds to give you the best education we could."

Anne hugged Marilla. "Thank you. I'll study as hard as I can and make you proud of me."

In the Queen's class were Anne, Gilbert, Ruby, Jane, and Josie Pye. They stayed after school every day to study for the entrance exam.

The rivalry between Anne and Gilbert was stronger than ever. But Gilbert paid no attention to Anne outside of class. He talked and laughed with the other girls. And sometimes he walked home with them. But he completely ignored Anne.

Anne did not like being ignored. But she knew it was her own fault. She didn't even feel angry at him anymore. She knew she had forgiven him and wanted to be his friend. But it was too late.

When the last day of school was over, Anne carried her textbooks up to the attic. She stacked them in an old trunk. Then she locked the trunk and threw the key into the blanket box.

"I'm not going to look at a textbook this whole vacation," she told Marilla. "I've studied as hard as I could all term. I just want to have fun this summer."

Anne went back to school in September, rested and ready to work hard again.

In March, Anne turned fifteen.

One day Marilla was amazed to find that Anne was taller than she was.

That night, Matthew came into the kitchen and was surprised to see Marilla crying. Marilla hardly ever cried.

"I was thinking about Anne," said Marilla. "She's growing up so fast. And she'll probably be away all next winter. I'll really miss her, Matthew."

"But she'll be able to come home often," Matthew said.

Marilla sighed. "It won't be the same as having her here all the time."

Anne was looking forward to going to Queen's. But she still had to pass the entrance exam.

In June she and her classmates went to Charlottetown to take the exam. Anne stayed with Miss Josephine Barry for the week.

Anne arrived home on Friday evening. She was tired, but she knew she had done the best she could on the exam.

"I think I did pretty well in everything except geometry," Anne told Diana. "I have a creepy feeling that I failed it."

"Oh, you'll pass all right," Diana said. "Don't worry."

But Anne wanted more than just to pass the exam. She wanted to come out ahead of Gilbert Blythe. She also wanted to be the best so that Matthew and Marilla would be proud of her.

Three weeks went by without a word.

Then, one day, Anne looked out her window and saw Diana running toward the house. She had a newspaper in her hand.

Moments later, Diana burst into the room.

"Anne, you passed!" she cried. "You passed the *very first!* You and Gilbert tied, but your name is first."

"I can't believe it," Anne whispered. "I hoped it would happen, but I never dreamed it really would."

Chapter 18
The Scholarship

Anne went off to Queen's Academy in the fall. Miss Barry found her a boarding-house to live in. Anne was very homesick for Green Gables at first. She was glad that Jane and Ruby—and even Josie Pye— were at Queen's, too.

Anne was able to go home or to Miss Barry's on weekends. And she made some new friends at school. Soon her homesickness wore off.

She studied hard, hoping to win a scholarship to Redmond College. There were two scholarships—the Medal and the Avery.

"I know I won't win the Avery," Anne said to Jane after the final exams were over. "Everyone says Emily Clay will get it. I'm not going to look at the bulletin board to see who won. You read it and then come and tell me. If I didn't win a scholarship, break it to me gently. Promise?"

Jane promised. The next moment, they saw a crowd of boys carrying Gilbert Blythe on their shoulders.

"Hooray for Blythe, Medalist!" they shouted.

Anne's heart sank. She had failed and Gilbert had won. She knew Matthew would be sorry. He had been so sure she would win.

And then somebody called out, "Three cheers for Anne Shirley, winner of the Avery!"

All the girls rushed up to Anne to congratulate her. Anne whispered to Jane, "Matthew and Marilla will be so pleased!

I have to write to them right away."

Matthew and Marilla came to Queen's for Anne's graduation. They watched proudly as Anne read the best essay.

"Reckon you're glad we kept her, Marilla?" whispered Matthew.

"It's not the first time I've been glad," Marilla snapped. "You do like to rub things in, Matthew Cuthbert."

Anne went home to Avonlea with Matthew and Marilla. Diana was at Green Gables to meet her.

"Oh, Diana, it's so good to be home again," Anne said. "And to see *you* again."

"Are you going to teach now that you've won the Avery?" Diana asked.

"No," said Anne. "I'm going to Redmond College in the fall. But first I'll have three wonderful months of vacation."

The next morning at breakfast, Anne asked Marilla, "Is Matthew all right? He looks as if he isn't feeling well."

"He's had a bad time with his heart,"

Marilla said. "I'm worried about him. He works too hard. Maybe he'll rest and get better now that you're home. You always cheer him up."

That evening, Anne went with Matthew to bring the cows to the back pasture.

"You've been working too hard," Anne said. "Why don't you take things easier?"

"I guess I just keep forgetting that I'm getting old," Matthew said.

"Today I wish I were the boy you and Marilla wanted," Anne said. "I could help you so much now."

"Well, I'd rather have you than a dozen boys," Matthew said. "It wasn't a boy who won the scholarship, was it? It was a girl— my girl."

Chapter 19
Difficult Times

"Matthew—Matthew—what is the matter? Matthew, are you sick?" Marilla asked.

Anne came into the kitchen. They both rushed toward Matthew. But before they could reach him, he fell to the floor.

"Anne, run for Martin—quick, quick!"

Martin, the hired man, hurried off for the doctor. But it was too late. Matthew was dead.

That night, Marilla heard Anne crying in her room. She went in to comfort her.

She put her arms around Anne and held her close. "There, there, don't cry so. It can't bring him back."

"Oh, Marilla, what will we do without him?" sobbed Anne.

"We've got each other," Marilla said gently. "I don't know what I'd do without you, Anne. I know I've been kind of strict and harsh with you. But I want you to know that I love you dearly. You've been my joy and comfort ever since you came to Green Gables."

Two days later, Matthew was buried. Then, slowly, life began to return to normal. But Anne still missed Matthew and thought of him often.

One evening, Anne and Marilla sat together on the front doorstep.

"Dr. Spencer was here today," Marilla said. "He wants me to see a special eye doctor in town tomorrow. I hope the doctor will give me the right kind of glasses. You won't mind staying here alone, will you?"

"I'll be all right," Anne said. "Diana will come over and keep me company. And don't worry. I won't get into any trouble."

Marilla laughed. "Do you remember the time you dyed your hair green?"

"I'll never forget it," Anne said with a smile. "I did feel bad about my red hair and freckles. Now my freckles are really gone! And people are nice enough to tell me my hair is auburn. Except for Josie Pye, of course."

Marilla went to town the next day and returned in the evening. She sat down at the kitchen table and put her head in her hands.

Anne was worried. "Are you tired, Marilla?" she asked.

"It's not that," Marilla said. She looked at Anne. "The eye doctor says I must give up all reading and sewing and any kind of work that strains my eyes. If I do that and wear the glasses he gave me, my eyes may not get any worse. But if I don't, he says I'll be blind in six months."

"But if you're careful, you won't lose your sight," Anne said. "And the new glasses may cure your headaches."

"What will I do if I can't read or sew or knit?" Marilla asked. "If I can't do those things, I might as well be blind!"

When Marilla went to bed, Anne sat at her window. She wondered what she could do to help Marilla. After a while, she found the answer.

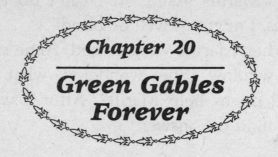

Chapter 20

Green Gables Forever

A few days later, Anne saw Marilla in the yard talking to a man. Marilla came back into the kitchen with tears in her eyes.

"He wants to buy Green Gables," said Marilla.

"Buy Green Gables?" Anne exclaimed. "Marilla, you're not going to sell Green Gables!"

"I have to," Marilla said. She began to cry. "I can't look after things here by myself. Especially if I lose my sight. I never thought I'd see the day when I'd have to sell my home."

"You can't sell Green Gables," Anne said firmly.

"I wish I didn't have to. But I can't stay here alone," sobbed Marilla.

"You won't have to stay here alone, Marilla," said Anne. "I'll be here with you. I'm not going to Redmond."

"Not going to Redmond!" Marilla lifted her face from her hands and stared at Anne. "What do you mean?"

"Just what I said. I'm not going to take the scholarship. I made up my mind the night you came back from the eye doctor. I would never leave you alone, after all you've done for me."

Anne took Marilla's hands in hers. "Let me tell you my plans. Mr. Barry wants to rent the farm next year. So you don't have to worry about that. And I'm going to teach at the Carmody school. I asked for the Avonlea school, but it's been promised to Gilbert Blythe. And I'll read to you and keep you cheered up."

"But you wanted to go to college," said Marilla.

"I'm going to keep on studying right here at home," Anne said. "And who knows? Maybe I will get to go to Redmond someday. But right now, saving Green Gables and helping you is more important."

Marilla smiled at Anne. "I guess I ought to make you go to college. But I know I can't, so I'm not going to try. I'll make it up to you, though."

Mrs. Lynde came up to Green Gables one evening with some news for Anne.

"The school board has decided to give you the Avonlea school," said Mrs. Lynde.

"But I thought they had promised it to Gilbert Blythe!" Anne exclaimed.

"So they did. But as soon as Gilbert heard that you wanted it, he decided not to take it. Then he gave them your name. He's going to teach over at White Sands."

"I'm not sure I ought to take it," said

Anne. "I don't think I should let Gilbert do that for me."

"It's already done," said Mrs. Lynde. "He's signed the papers for the White Sands school. It won't do him any good if you turn down the Avonlea school. So you might as well take it."

The next evening, Anne went to put flowers on Matthew's grave.

On her way home she saw Gilbert Blythe coming toward her. He lifted his cap when he saw her. But he would have walked right by if Anne had not stopped and held out her hand.

Gilbert took her hand eagerly.

"Gilbert," Anne said, her cheeks red, "I want to thank you for giving up the school for me. It was very nice of you— and I want you to know that I appreciate it."

"I was happy to be able to do it," said Gilbert. "Are we going to be friends after this? Have you really forgiven me at last?"

Anne laughed. "I forgave you that day by the pond landing. But I didn't know it. I've been sorry ever since."

"We're going to be the best of friends," Gilbert said, smiling. "We were born to be good friends. Come on, I'm going to walk home with you."

When Anne entered the kitchen, Marilla looked at her curiously.

"Who came up the lane with you?" she asked.

"Gilbert Blythe," said Anne. "I met him on Barry's hill."

"I didn't know you and Gilbert were such good friends that you'd talk to him for half an hour at the gate," Marilla said with a smile.

"Were we really there for half an hour?" said Anne. "It seemed like just a few minutes. But, you see, we have five years of lost friendship to catch up on, Marilla."

Anne sat at her window for a long time

that night. The wind purred in the cherry and apple trees around the house. The stars twinkled above the fir trees in the hollow. She could see Diana's light in the distance.

Anne was happy about the future. She would study and teach. She would have good times with her friends.

And she and Marilla would always have a home at Green Gables.

Deborah G. Felder is the author of many books and magazine articles. She loves to travel, and one of her favorite things to do is visit the places she reads about in books. She and her husband live in Connecticut with their cat, Lily.

Lucy Maud Montgomery was born in 1874 in Canada, on Prince Edward Island, which is the setting for all of her "Anne" books. *Anne of Green Gables* was published in 1908. Translated into seventeen languages, it has become a classic around the world. Anne has also come to life on TV and in several movies and plays.